Licensed exclusively to Top That Publishing Ltd
Tide Mill Way, Woodbridge, Suffolk, IP12 1AP, UK
www.topthatpublishing.com
Copyright © 2014 Tide Mill Media
All rights reserved
0 2 4 6 8 9 7 5 3 1
Printed and bound in China

ISBN 978-1-78445-025-0

A catalogue record for this book is available from the British Library

HORACE HORSE

Horace the Horse was lost.
He and his friends had been moved to a new barn, but
Horace had stopped to nibble some grass on the way.

Now his friends were nowhere to be seen.

Horace set off to find his friends.
'There's one!' he whinnied, galloping over
to a children's playground.

But it was only a pretend horse on a spring.
'Is this my home?' he asked.

'NAY! NAY! NAY!'

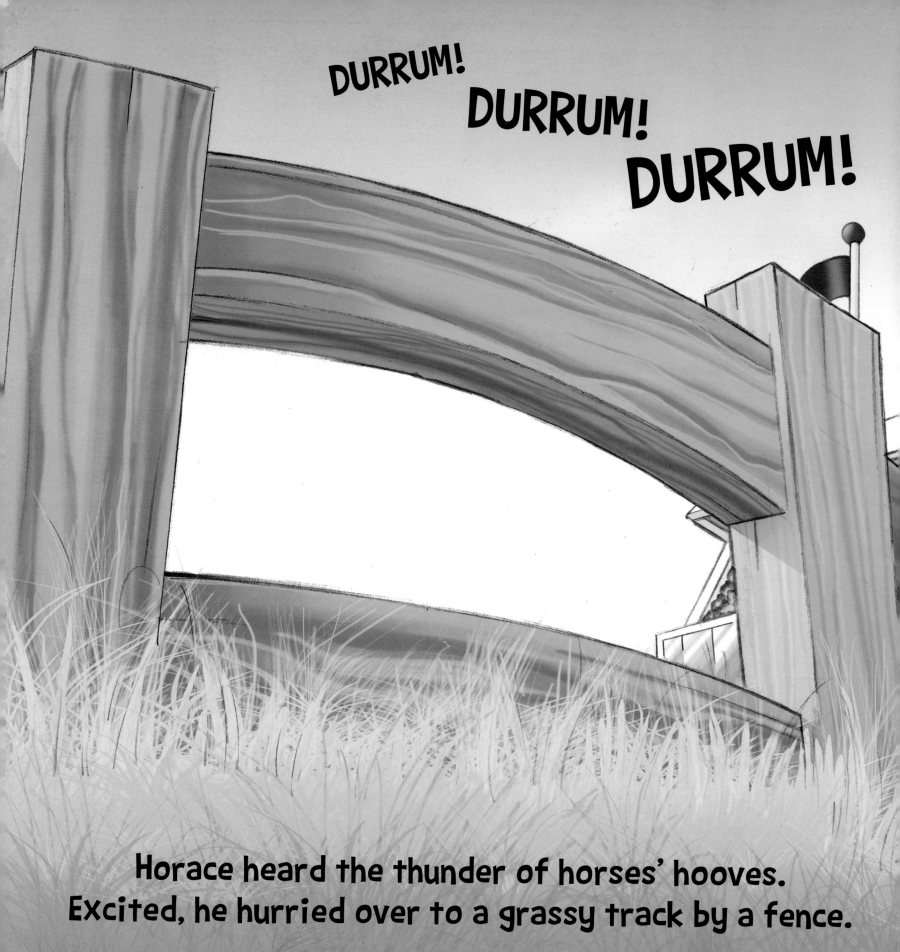

Horace heard the thunder of horses' hooves.
Excited, he hurried over to a grassy track by a fence.

'My friends are coming!' he chuckled.

But it wasn't Horace's friends.
It was racehorses on a racetrack.
They galloped past, smothering him in dust and stones.

Then Horace spotted some horses in the distance.
They seemed to be jumping a hedge.

'My friends are out for a run!'
he said with a big, happy smile.

Horace hurried around the hedge and found himself at a funfair. All of the horses were wooden, going up and down on a carousel!

'Is this my home?' he sighed, miserably.

'NAY! NAY! NAY!'

Horace wandered on and on in search
of his friends, but he couldn't find them.
Then, it started to rain.

'I'll shelter in here,' he thought, trotting into a big, empty barn.

Soon Horace heard the clatter of hooves. Looking up, he saw all of his friends coming to greet him. He had sheltered in his new barn!